First published in the United States and Canada in 2018 by NorthSouth Books, Inc.,
an imprint of NordSüd Verlag AG, CH-8050 Zürich, Switzerland.

Distributed in the United States by NorthSouth Books, Inc., New York 10016.
Library of Congress Cataloging-in-Publication Data is available.

ISBN: 978-0-7358-4319-6
Printed in Latvia 2017
1 3 5 7 9 · 10 8 6 4 2
www.northsouth.com

MIX
Paper from
responsible sources
FSC® C002795
FSC
www.fsc.org

The Tiger's Egg

by Nele Brönner

North
South

Herman prowled around his enclosure. He was in a very bad mood.
The kudu and the gnu had been trying to prove which of them was stronger.
"Why do I have to be surrounded by all these show-offs?" he growled,
dipping his paw in the moat and frightening the fish.

Herman lay down on the roof of his tiger house. It was more peaceful up there.

Plink! Something fell on his head. "How dare they throw things at me!" he growled.

But what rolled down between Herman's paws didn't look like a pebble. It was small, pretty, and oval shaped.

"Maybe it's an egg?" Herman looked up. But he didn't see any nests or birds.

"I'll look after you until someone comes," murmured Herman, and very carefully he wrapped his soft, furry tail around the egg.

"Nobody will dare lay a claw on a tiger egg." And he happily fell asleep.

The next morning Herman collected a few pieces of straw and built a little nest. Then he plucked the softest hairs from his chest and carefully put the egg in the now-cushioned hollow of the nest.

When he was quite certain that nobody was looking, he pushed the nest under a bush and trotted away to have his breakfast.

When Herman came back, there was something wrong with the egg.
There was a crack in it.

"Who would do such a thing?" he asked angrily. "A poor defenseless egg . . ."

Tenderly he licked the shell. Then he felt something move inside the egg. . . .

"Aha!" he thought. "Whatever's in the egg is trying to hatch. That's what is
happening." He'd heard all about it from the ducks that sometimes bathed in
his moat.

Herman heard a soft tapping from inside the egg. Then a clicking and a kicking.
The egg fell over on its side, and then suddenly it broke open.
Out came a tiny wet bird with enormous feet.
It looked at Herman. "CHEEP!" said the baby bird with his beak very wide open.
"He wants something to eat," Herman said to himself, and he went off to hunt.

All day long the old tiger was busy catching grasshoppers, beetles, larvae, caterpillars, flies, worms, spiders, and a tick. The little bird gobbled them all up.

"What are you looking for?" the pink ape called out.

But Herman didn't feel like answering.

"It's better if nobody knows about you," he said to the tiny bird. He gazed at him for a moment. "You look like a very small, very soft little tiger."

The bird said something that sounded almost like "Herman."

The next day the baby bird tottered along the edge of his nest on his thin little legs.

"I want to go hunting with you," he squeaked. "I'm a tiger too."

"No, no," said Herman. "It's too dangerous. There are lots of animals out there that could eat you."

"Will they eat you too?" asked the bird, eyes wide.

"Me? Nobody eats me!" growled Herman. "I only need to let out one terrible tiger roar and they're all scared stiff."

"Good," said the baby bird, "then teach me how to do a terrible tiger roar."

"Hm ... well ... let's see," said Herman. "Stand like me, with your legs apart ... take a deep breath ... now open your mouth wide and say as loud as you can, 'ROOOAAARRR!'"

Herman roared so loud that the leaves trembled on the trees and the baby bird fell out of the nest. "Wow, that was terrific!" he peeped.

"Now it's your turn. First stand with your legs apart, fluff up your neck feathers, and pull your eyebrows together so you look really nasty. Very good. As terrifying as a tiger."

"Tweet!" cheeped the little bird, and opened his beak as wide as he could.

"Tweet! Tweeeeeet! Is that good, Herman? Am I a dangerous tiger too?"

Herman nodded and grinned.

Roaring makes you hungry, and so Herman went to hunt for more insects.

"Bring me some ants!" cheeped the bird.

"Get back inside your nest and keep very still, little tiger," said Herman, and disappeared into the bamboo.

When Herman returned, the nest was empty.

"Little tiger," called Herman, "where are you?"

What he saw took his breath away. The little bird was hopping through the iron bars. All the time he kept saying a loud and cheerful "Tweet! Tweeeeet!"

Suddenly Herman saw the big gray pelican striding along with its long beak wide open.

"Quick! Come back! Hop through the railings, little bird!" screeched Herman.

The little bird saw the pelican. But he didn't hop back through the railings.
He got into position. Just as he had learned to do: legs apart, feathers puffed up,
angry expression, and then a loud "TWEEEEEEEEET!" straight at the pelican.

"Oh no! What have I done?" The horrified Herman held his paws in front of
his face. "That crazy bird really thinks he's a tiger!"

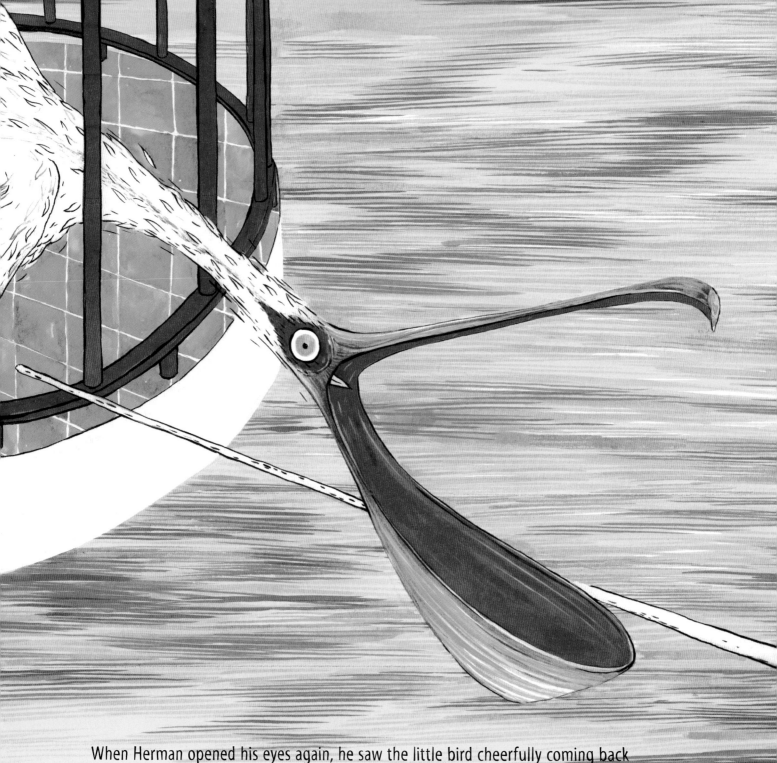

When Herman opened his eyes again, he saw the little bird cheerfully coming back
through the bars.

"Did you see that?" he cheeped.

The pelican stuck its long neck through the railing and snapped at the empty air.
The little bird was long since across the moat.

"I scared him stiff!" the bird squeaked with delight. Herman caught him in his
trembling paws.

"Oh, you amazingly brave tiger bird, that was so dangerous! You should stay in the nest!"

"But didn't you hear me roar?" squeaked the little bird. "I gave that great big bird the
shock of his life!"

Herman nodded and sighed. "Oh dear, I need to make him understand that I really am a big tiger and he's only a little tiger bird who just looks a tiny bit like a tiger. Even that old, deaf pelican could have eaten him up!"

Herman gave the little bird a sort of rough but gentle kiss. "Tomorrow," he murmured to himself. "I'll tell him tomorrow. We've had enough excitement for one day."